LOVE

IN THE TIME OF

ERECTILE DYSFUNCTION

A Short Story

by

George Lindamood

Author of

The Accidental Peacemaker

ISBN: 9798577542184

Cover design: Magdalena Bassett
Cover illustration: Albert Maier

COMPULSORY PREFACE

(THIS MEANS YOU.)

Eight years ago, I wrote this story as my contribution to a local writing circle. Along with the amusement I had intended to evoke, it caused a certain amount of puzzlement as to why I would write something like this, but the late Jim Fisher, Professor of English at Peninsula College (Port Angeles, WA), answered that as he tagged my tale for what it is — a shaggy dog story.

Now that Donald Trump's presidency has come and gone, Fisher's insight may help us understand Trump's administration — and perhaps his whole life as well — for what it was, *a real-life shaggy dog story*.

According to Wikipedia,

In its original sense, a *shaggy dog story* is an extremely long-winded anecdote characterized by extensive narration of typically irrelevant incidents and terminated by an anticlimax. Shaggy dog stories play upon the audience's preconceptions of joke-telling. The audience listens to the story with certain expectations, which are either simply not met or met in some entirely unexpected manner. A lengthy shaggy dog story derives its humor from the fact that the joke-teller held the attention of the listeners for a long time for no reason at all, as the end resolution is essentially meaningless.

George
Lindamood

Disclaimer

Gabriel García Márquez was a real person and the quotes, direct and indirect, from his novel *Love in the Time of Cholera* (English language translation, Everyman's Library, 1997) are authentic. Burt Bacharach, Hal David, Cole Porter, and Richard Strauss are or were real persons too, and they really did write the music attributed to them herein. Pfizer and Upjohn are the names of present and former companies, respectively; and *Viagra*, *Cialis*, and *Levitra* are the registered trade names of actual drugs used to treat erectile dysfunction (ED). Everything else in this story is fictional, and any re-semblance to actual persons, products, or-ganizations, or situations is completely co-incidental.

IN APPRECIATION

To Gabo,
with thanks for his inspiration
and
apologies for my impertinence.

The art of love ...

is largely

the art of persistence.

— Albert Ellis (1913-2007),
American psychologist

LOVE
IN THE TIME OF
ERECTILE DYSFUNCTION

I've always wanted to be a writer, a good writer, maybe even a great writer. The ambition ambushed me in a sophomore course on Modern Literature, when I read *Love in the Time of Cholera* by 1982 Nobel laureate Gabriel García Márquez.

At first I was skeptical about the book, almost hostile. "What do I care about love between a couple of old farts," I snorted. "It's right there in the book, where the heroine's middle-age daughter says, 'Love is ridiculous at our age, but at theirs it is revolting.'" However, by the time I finished reading, I was captivated not only by the author's literary style, even in translation, but also by the story itself. It's as if I had fallen in love with the idea of being in love.

Anyhow, I decided to guide my life along the path of Garcia Márquez' story, as close as I could reasonably come to that in Williamstown, the small river port in southeastern Ohio where I grew up. My first objective was to pick the 'right' person to love: somebody beautiful, charming, and graceful, of course — but most of all, somebody slightly beyond my reach, so that success would not come quickly or easily, if at all. This, I thought, would consign me to at least a couple

decades, if not a lifetime, of unrequit-
ed love like that of *Cholera's* hero,
Florentino Ariza, thereby inspiring me
to write, in my fifties, my own *Great
American Novel*.

It didn't take me long to identify
an unreachable heartthrob. There was
really only one candidate: Jessica
Haines, who was then still enrolled in
the local high school. 'Jess' had
caught my eye when I too was a stu-
dent at Williamstown High. She had
been my date at a few school proms,
but she had never seemed as attracted

to me as I was to her, per-haps because of the two years difference in our ages and maturity. And by the time I graduated, she was 'going steady' with her classmate, Mark Moyers, the star running back on the WHS football team, and rumor had it that they planned to marry right after their graduation.

Accordingly, my early love life was unfulfilling although not exactly ascetic, sparsely populated with various coeds I met at Williamstown College. It wasn't until I was in grad school at Ohio State University that utter loneliness finally drove me to marry. It wasn't a great marriage, but it promised to be a decent one, providing the utmost opportunity if not the maximum temptation. In time, however, even the opportunity faded, leading me to recall the *Cholera* line that after many years of marriage some women seem to have three periods per week. Thus, I began to look elsewhere to satisfy my 'venereal appetites,' as García Márquez tastefully denoted them, and within a few years the inevitable divorce ensued.

Now I was interjected into the milieu of Florentino Ariza, free to feast at a veritable smorgasbord of divorcées, widows, and even spinsters, all seeking remnants of love's warmth before their allure evaporated altogether. I found the 'ridiculous' promiscuity of middle age invigorating but at the same time depressing, because of the shallowness imposed by the sheer number and variety of relationships. (Florentino Ariza filled some twenty-five notebooks, with six-hundred-twenty-two entries of long-term liaisons, apart from his countless fleeting adventures that didn't deserve even a charitable note.) Nevertheless, I drew strength from the hope that my beloved Jess might also have fallen from the grace of her marriage like so many of my casual consorts, and my mother unwittingly sustained that fantasy with her occasional reports of chance meetings with Jessica when she came home to visit her parents.

As I turned the page from forty-nine to fifty, my persistence was rewarded when Mom telephoned to wish me a Happy Birthday. "I ran into Jessica in the supermarket yesterday," she said. "She's come back to Williamstown to look after her parents, who are going into an assisted-living apartment. Both of her kids are now in college, and she's split up with her husband because he wants to stay in Texas." My heart leapt for joy, and I immediately scheduled a week's vacation so I could return to my hometown and immerse myself in the happiness of pursuit under the guise of looking after my own mother.

I contacted the English Department at Williamstown College to see if there were any faculty vacancies. There was one, of sorts: a one-year, non-tenure-track Lecturer position to fill in for a senior professor who was going on sabbatical. It wasn't what I had hoped for, but I submitted my application and scheduled an interview with the department chairperson during my imminent hometown visit.

The chairperson was sympathetic to my expressed need to care for my aging mother, even to the point of suggesting that I also contact the local community college regarding vacancies there. Over the next month, the pieces fell into place — at least most of them. I was offered the Lectureship at my *alma mater*, and I quickly accepted. The pay was significantly less than what I had been making as a technical writer in Baltimore, but I figured that the cost-of-living would be lower in Williamstown, and I hoped to supplement my income with some free-lance writing. If that didn't pan out, my fall-back plan was to get started on my *Great American Novel*.

With that settled, I concentrated my energies on the real purpose for my abrupt career change: reconnecting with my secret love, Jessica. There, however, the pieces remained scattered. I interrogated my mother in an attempt to determine precisely where and when she had previously encountered Jess, but I had to be circumspect so as not to reveal my more-than-casual interest. Then I made a point of going shopping — daily! — at the supermarket Mom identified, at about the time of day when she had seen Jess. The odds of finding Jess were slim, but on the ninth day luck was with me and I successfully contrived to 'bump into' her as she was wheeling her grocery cart out the door. She gave me a big smile and greeted me warmly, so we spent some ten minutes exchanging vague details about our lives over the thirty-some years since we had last met. Without giving any hint of my ulterior motives, I eventually steered the conversation to where I dared ask her to meet me for coffee, and she readily agreed, innocently supplying her phone number. Afterward I was concerned that I had seemed uptight and unbalanced, thereby raising 'caution flags' that would subvert my plans to re-establish our friendship, a friendship I fervently hoped would soon blossom into all-out love. But if Jess had had any sense of foreboding as we talked, she hid it well, giving the impression that she was genuinely happy that I had moved back to Williamstown.

Thus began what was in my mind a prolonged seduction, one I'd waited for, longed for, and fantasized about for more than thirty years. No, it was not the fifty-one years, nine months, and four days that Florentino Ariza waited for access to his beloved in Garcia Márquez' novel, but that story took place in a very different culture, Colombia, nearly a century ago. But like Florentino Ariza's subsequent pursuit of Fermina Daza, my seduction of Jess stretched out almost two years, during which I consolidated my professional situation as a full-time teacher at the Muskingum Community College, while she took a receptionist job at a local furniture manufacturer. Meanwhile, our dates followed the usual progression — long chats over coffee, next movies and concerts, then dinners and dancing — but it wasn't until she quietly mentioned over after-dinner sherry one evening that her divorce had recently been finalized, that I summoned the courage to try for a good-night kiss. She readily acquiesced, and although it lacked passion, it was sufficient to launch me into a new level of fantasizing and scheming to get her into bed.

In the months since I had returned to Williamstown, my bedtime hours had been quite solitary — not that there weren't available partners if I had aggressively sought them out, but I didn't want to do anything that might alienate Jess if she had somehow gotten wind of it. When I finally invited her to my apartment for post-dinner coffee and conversation a few weeks later, a playful kiss escalated into one of surprising intensity, followed by a tight embrace and heavy breathing. I was more than ready for that but totally unprepared for what happened next — or, to be more accurate, what *didn't* happen. I certainly had no reason to expect anything like that — after all, I was in excellent health and good physical condition, thanks to regular exercise and a sensible diet, and I had never, ever had the slightest problem with 'being ready,' as the endless TV ads for *Viagra*, *Cialis*, and *Levitra* euphemistically characterized the situation.

Despite the surprise, Jess handled it all with charm and grace, smiling and saying something about "both of us being out of practice," and suggesting that we "try again" on next week's date. So we did, but the result was the same — and again on the date after that, and the date after that. I did my level best to improvise, using my touch and tongue to give her pleasure, and she attempted to reciprocate, although her knowledge of what makes men tick was apparently limited to what she had experienced in more than twenty years of straight-laced marriage to a Tarzanesque jock. The bottom line was that my batting average became 'oh-for-nine,' and I seemed destined for perpetual no-hitters.

I scheduled a hurry-up visit to a urologist, who could find no physiological reason for The Problem, especially since I reported that my organ rose with the sun every day. I nodded my head in understanding as the doctor explained that the cause was insufficient blood supply to my penis, and I listened with rapt attention as he identified three possible approaches to The Solution: chemical, as with prescription drugs like *Viagra* or traditional folk remedies such as ginseng, goat weed, and powdered walnuts;

physical, as with vacuum devices for which Medicare paid more than a quarter *billion* dollars in the past decade ($47 million in 2010 alone); and psycho-spiritual, ranging from sex therapists and psychologists to undocumented counseling, prayers, and exorcisms by ministers and witch doctors. Rather than choose a course of treatment on the spot, I said I wanted time to explore the options, especially the contraindications and costs. Then I wisely decided to talk it all out with Jess.

Again, she was the quintessence of compassion, expressing her lasting commitment to me and her appreciation for my openness in sharing the matter with her, but she concluded by professing near-total ignorance, something that reminded me of a line in *Cholera*, uttered by the heroine Fermina Daza on her wedding night: "I have never been able to understand how that thing works." That immediately led me to reject the penis pump option, and it called into question the suitability of drugs like *Viagra*, even if the caution of "dangerous side-effects such as an erection lasting more than four hours" was probably more the doing of marketing managers than liability lawyers. That left the psycho-spiritual approach as the preferred option.

Perhaps fortuitously, licensed sex therapists were nowhere to be found in a burg as small as Williamstown, and psychologists weren't in abundance either. So I decided to see what I could do on my own, with Jessica's sympathetic, if none-too-knowledge-able, support. I began with the observation, attributed to the comedian Robin Williams, that "God gave men both a penis and a brain, but unfortunately not enough blood supply to run both at the same time." From that, it was perfectly obvious — to me, anyhow — that the needs of my penis could be satisfied only by diverting blood from my brain. "It's simply a 'zero-sum game,'" I reasoned in a rare moment of genius. "It is also the basic logic underlying women's fashions throughout history as well as virtually all modern advertising, so there is a considerable corpus of knowledge of how to effect this diversion and, more importantly, how to do so without causing permanent damage to the brain — not that the fashion and advertising industries give a damn about that." After exhaustive and exhausting study of this corpus, I carefully extracted what I felt was the hidden essence and incorporated it into my own methodology.

Rather than compel my brain to relinquish its blood for urgent service elsewhere as the chemical and physical treatments do, I sought to seduce — an apt metaphor, I thought — my brain into willingly sharing some of its blood supply through a simple process of conditioning. I began by rocking myself in a single-seat playground swing that I bought and reinforced to take my weight, combining centrifugal force and gravity to coax blood to the nether parts of my body. I also applied other physical stimuli — vibration and warm air — to improve circulation in the groin area. At the same time, I played music to set the mood — songs like *What the World Needs Now Is Love* by Hal David and Burt Bacharach and *Let's Do It* by Cole Porter — and displayed images on a large computer screen that hinted at love and/or sexual activity. Interlaced in the images were tachistoscopic shots of male and female genitalia, each lasting only a fraction of a second, in a carefully arranged sequence building into explicit sexual activity as the music swelled into an energetic, blood-stirring strain and ended in a frenetic climax. With two weeks of daily hour-long sessions in this regimen, I was able to program my brain — the part that was still functioning with blood becoming ever scarcer — to associate sexual arousal and activity with the music.

It worked beautifully! Soon Jess and I had consummated our relationship and were re-enacting our success quite frequently (although my neighbors began complaining about the loud music at odd hours). I proceeded to teach her what Garcia Márquez so vividly portrayed: "that nothing one does in bed is immoral if it helps to perpetuate love," and she responded by demonstrating that "when a woman decides to sleep with a man, there is no wall she will not scale, no fortress she will not destroy, no moral consideration she will not ignore at its very root: there is no God worth worrying about." I had achieved my life's goal!

However, there were some unanticipated side effects to my therapy. Whenever I heard the climactic music I had programmed into my conditioned stimulus, my body would *always* react with the conditioned response, *no matter what the situation.* This led to an exceedingly embarrassing incident when a visiting orchestra played Richard Strauss's *Also Sprach Zarathustra* at a Community Concert.

Nevertheless, I was happy, so deliriously happy — I wasn't content to rest on my laurels. I continued to refine my methodology, not only for my personal use but also so that I could share it with others. Then I opened a somewhat covert sex therapy practice, advertised only through word-of-mouth from satisfied patients. Eventually, news of it got back to local psychologists and urologists who, realizing that the health risks were almost non-existent, overcame their initial skepticism and began referring clients to me. Within a year, Jess and I got married, and she joined me in running an 'ED clinic,' focusing on the heart, not the glands.

A few years later, I gave up my writing and teaching career, forsaking the dream of becoming Gabriel García Márquez' literary successor but laughing all the way to the bank (between trips to the bedroom with Jess). And after several more increasingly successful and lucrative years in business, I retired from active practice and sold the rights to my technique for a

considerable sum. Curiously enough,
the buyer was the pharmaceutical
firm, Pfizer. I half expected that Pfizer
would simply bury my enterprise so
as to maximize their revenue from *Viagra*, but Pfizer's MBAs surprised
me: they created a new subsidiary to
market the therapy under the name of
an old-line drug firm that Pfizer had
acquired some years ago. The compa-
ny was Upjohn.

About the Author

George Lindamood was born and raised in Marietta, Ohio. Since retiring from a forty-two year career in information technology, he has served as an AmeriCorps volunteer, taught English in China, earned a doctorate in religious studies, and built a fine local reputation as a church and jazz musician. Most recently, he has turned his attention to writing fiction and poetry. He and his wife Annette live on the Olympic Peninsula in Washington.

Also by George Lindamood

The Accidental Peacemaker, a full-length novel, published December 2012, available in all e-book formats from Amazon, SmashWords, and other e-book sellers, and in paperback from Amazon and other on-line and local booksellers.

Some reader comments:

"Reading *The Accidental Peacemaker* by George Lindamood over Holiday Break provided a much-needed escape…. I stayed in the Oregon woods for a week; the characters and insights from the book remain with me…. I highly recommend this well-written, well-plotted, thoughtful novel."

"Lindamood writes with the penetrating insights gained in all his years of experience…. We want to keep reading because we care about the characters, and want to know what each surprising turn of events will bring."

"Reality is surreal in this Northwest community. As the reader, you'll win a spiritual lottery and come to understand our world a little better."

"It's refreshing to read a spiritual story that has not been sanitized of human life-force impulses."

"I was amazed, dazed, taken aback, bowled over, and blown away! I'm recommending [the book] to all my family and everyone I know."

"Damn good!"

Also by George Lindamood

9½ *Maxims for Wisdom Study*, *Guidance for the Spiritually Adventurous*, co-authored with Annette Lindamood, published in 2020 in paper-back only. For those intrepid beings who are spiritually adventurous, wisdom study can provide meaning and comfort at any point in life, but especially in the latter years when youthful ambitions are compromised by failing energies and acuity. This small book is a primer for that period but also possibly earlier. It was compiled and written by two octogenarian teachers who have traveled, studied, and experienced perhaps a little more than their peers and who are thus motivated to find meaning by "giving back." Perhaps it will help you, the reader, find greater meaning and joy in your life, too.

Printed in Great Britain
by Amazon

29709603R00026